YOUR TURN, MY TU

PLAYSKOOL

Drip, Drop!
The Rain Won't Stop!

by Sheila Sweeny Higginson   illustrated by Josie Yee

Simon Spotlight
New York London Toronto Sydney

SIMON SPOTLIGHT
An imprint of Simon & Schuster Children's Publishing Division
1230 Avenue of the Americas, New York, New York 10020
For information about special discounts for bulk purchases, please contact Simon &
Schuster Special Sales at 1-866-506-1949 or business@simonandschuster.com.
Manufactured in the United States of America 1109 LAK
First Edition
2 4 6 8 10 9 7 5 3 1
Library of Congress Cataloging-in-Publication Data
Higginson, Sheila Sweeny, 1966–
Drip, drop! The rain won't stop! / by Sheila Sweeny Higginson. — 1st ed.
p. cm. — (Your turn, my turn reader)
At head of title: Playskool
ISBN 978-1-4169-9046-8 (alk. paper)
I. Playskool. II. Title. III. Title: Drip, drop! The rain will not stop! IV. Title: Playskool.
PZ7.H537Dri 2010
[E]—dc22
2009012168

Digger the Dog loves to play.

Today he wants to play outside.

He wants to build

a giant castle

in the sandbox!

Digger grabs his pail and shovel.

He is ready to dig, dig, dig,

and build, build, build!

Digger looks outside.

"It is raining!" he cries.

"I cannot play outside today.

I cannot build my castle

in the sandbox."

YOUR TURN

Drip, drop.

Drip, drop.

The rain is falling. *Drip, drop!*

RAINBOW ALERT!

Can you find the colorful rainbow hidden somewhere on these pages?

Ding, dong!

It is Go Go Dino!

"Want to play inside with me
on this rainy day?" Go Go asks.

"Okay," says Digger.

But Digger is not happy.

He wanted to build
a castle in the sandbox today.

Plip, plop.

Plip, plop.

The rain is falling. *Plip, plop!*

Can you find the colorful rainbow hidden somewhere on these pages?

Go Go takes out blocks.

He stacks them up.

They fall down.

Digger builds them up again.

But Digger is not happy.

He wanted to build

a castle in the sandbox today.

Splish, splash.

Splish, splash.

The rain is falling. *Splish, splash!*

RAINBOW ALERT!

Can you find the colorful rainbow hidden somewhere on these pages?

Go Go sees some paper.

He cuts it up.

Digger glues the pieces down.

He makes a pretty picture.

But Digger is not happy.

He wanted to build

a castle in the sandbox today.

Pitter, patter.

Pitter, patter.

The rain is falling. *Pitter, patter!*

Can you find the colorful rainbow hidden somewhere on these pages?

Go Go is hungry.

Digger finds some bread.

Go Go spreads some jam on it.

Digger cuts the bread into shapes.

It is a yummy snack.

But Digger is not happy.

He wanted to build

a castle in the sandbox today.

Drip, drop.

Drip, drop.

The rain is falling. *Drip, drop!*

Can you find the colorful rainbow hidden somewhere on these pages?

Go Go finds some boxes.

He stacks them up.

Digger draws some doors.

Then he draws some windows.

But Digger is not happy.

He wanted to build

a castle in the sandbox today.

Plip, plop.

Plip, plop.

The rain is falling. *Plip, plop!*

Can you find the colorful rainbow
hidden somewhere on these pages?

Go Go has two chairs.

He also has a blanket.

Digger puts the blanket

on top of the chairs.

Digger and Go Go crawl inside.

But Digger is not happy.

He wanted to build

a castle in the sandbox today.

Splish, splash.
Splish, splash.
The rain is falling. *Splish, splash!*

Can you find the colorful rainbow
hidden somewhere on these pages?

Go Go crawls out
from under the blanket.
Go Go wonders why
Digger is not happy.
"I am having fun," Go Go says.
"But you are not."

Pitter, patter.
Pitter, patter.
The rain is falling. *Pitter, patter!*

RAINBOW ALERT!

Can you find the colorful rainbow hidden somewhere on these pages?

"I am sorry," says Digger.
"I wanted to play outside
    in the sandbox today.
    I wanted to build a castle."
"Digger, look!" Go Go says.
"You have built lots and lots
    of castles today!"

Drip, drop.

Drip, drop.

The rain is **STOPPING.** *Drip, drop!*

RAINBOW ALERT!

Can you find the colorful rainbow hidden somewhere on these pages?

Digger smiles.

"You are right, Go Go!" he says.

"And guess what?" says Go Go.

"The rain is stopping."

"Let's go make one more castle," says
Digger.

Hip, hip, hooray!
Hip, hip, hooray!
Now we can go outside to play!

RAINBOW ALERT!

Can you find the colorful rainbow hidden somewhere on these pages?

Digger grabs his pail.

Go Go grabs the shovel.

They dig, dig, dig,

and build, build, build.

They make a muddy castle

in the sandbox.

Digger and Go Go are very happy.

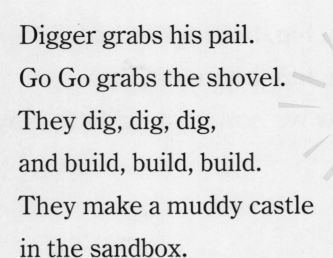